Balinese Children's Favorite Stories

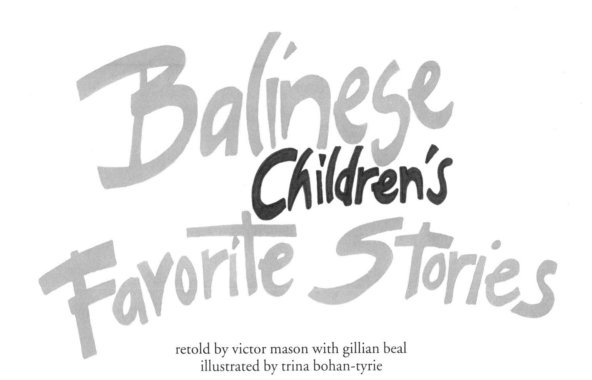

Balinese Children's Favorite Stories

retold by victor mason with gillian beal
illustrated by trina bohan-tyrie

PERIPLUS EDITIONS
Singapore • Hong Kong • Indonesia

The Balinese have a rich oral tradition. All the stories in this book have been handed down from one generation to the next and many are still told in Bali today. But their origin is obscure.

Some of the tales are clearly taken from the Fables of Aesop, here freshly retold in a Balinese setting. Aesop himself is an unknown—some believe his name was a *nom de plume* of an anonymous author, others think he may have been a Phrygian slave of the Romans; in any case all his tales teach us that pride goes before a fall, that humility is a virtue, and vanity a folly.

For some of the other stories, I simply could not find a source. The simpleton and the effete young rajah, for example, and the tale of the two sisters, are all peculiarly Balinese—but to my knowledge they have never been written down. I have seen them, or parts of them, enacted on the stage in Balinese Gambuh and Ardja performances, and they are part of the vast repertory of Balinese tantric tales which are derived from a common source somewhere between Europe and Asia—but of written records, I found none.

I would like to thank Dewa Nyoman Batuan from Pengosekan in the Regency of Gianyar; and Pak Dewe, who gave me the ingredients for these tales over 30 years ago. Without him, there would have been nothing to write about— and no book at all.

I hereby dedicate this book to my grand- children, Arjun and Natasha.

– Victor Mason

Published by Periplus Editions (HK) Ltd.

www.periplus.com

Text Copyright © 2001 Victor Mason
Illustrations Copyright © 2001 Trina Bohan-Tyrie

LCC Card No. 99505584
ISBN 978-0-7946-0740-1
Printed in Malaysia

Editors Kim Inglis, Jocelyn Lau; production Violet Wong

18 17 16 15 14 13   10 9 8 7 6 5 4 3 2 1   1301TWP

Distributed by:

North America, Latin America and Europe Tuttle Publishing,
364 Innovation Drive, North Clarendon, VT 05759-9436, USA
Tel: 1 (802) 773 8930; Fax: 1 (802) 773 6993
Email: info@tuttlepublishing.com Website: www.tuttlepublishing.com

Asia Pacific Berkeley Books Pte Ltd, 61 Tai Seng Avenue, #02-12
Singapore 534167. Tel: (65) 6280 1330; Fax: (65) 6280 6290
Email: inquires@periplus.com.sg Website: www.periplus.com

Japan Tuttle Publishing, Yaekari Building, 3F,
5-4-12 Osaki, Shinagawa-ku, Tokyo 141-0032, Japan
Tel: (81) 3 5437 0171 Fax: (81) 3 5437 0755
Email: sales@tuttle.co.jp; www. tuttle.co.jp

Indonesia PT Java Books Indonesia, Jl Rawa Gelam IV No. 9
Kawasan Industri Pulogadung, Jakarta 13930, Indonesia
Tel: (62) 21 4682 1088; Fax: (62) 21 461 0206
Email: crm@periplus.co.id Website: www.periplus.com

Contents

The Haughty Toad

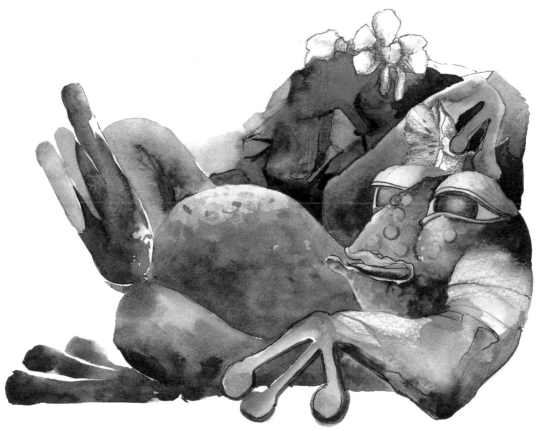

In a dark corner of a beautiful tropical garden, heavy with the scent of frangipani flowers, there once lived a mean and nasty toad. Gobrag was his name and he was a very ugly toad indeed. He had a stout body, short legs and a rough, warty skin.

Most of the time Gobrag just sat beneath the stones, blinking his eyes disdainfully. Sometimes he would blurt out a deep throaty croak that disturbed the peace of the garden. Every now and then, with a great show of self-importance, he would glower at some beast that happened to pass by, and noisily gulp great lungfuls of air. His body would then grow so broad and round that it seemed ready to burst.

Gobrag did this because he had a very high opinion of himself. He was a haughty fellow indeed. He felt far superior to the earthworms that crawled their way through the earth. He thought he was better than the crickets that chirped gaily when the sun went down. He believed himself to be a cut above the black and yellow spiders that wove their intricate webs between the palm trees.

Above all, Gobrag deemed himself more talented, more sophisticated and more important than·a group of frogs who gathered daily at the garden pond.

These gentle frogs were totally unlike Gobrag. They were bright green in colour and had big, beautiful eyes. Every day they settled on the pond's large lily pads and sang a tuneful chorus that entertained all the other creatures in the garden.

But as soon as they began singing, a loud, irritating noise would come from the corner where Gobrag lived.
"*Gooooo, brrrr, aaaa gggghhh!*" he would begin in his raucous voice, and continue:

"As East is East, and West is West,
I am the biggest and I am the best!"

After saying this Gobrag would puff himself up, look very pleased with himself and repeat his rhyme over and over, much to the annoyance of the little frogs.

They tried to ignore Gobrag and carry on singing, but his awful croaking just grew louder and louder until they couldn't even hear themselves think!
Then they tried moving to a far corner of the garden. But Gobrag's noise still carried through the air and disturbed them. Then they tried waiting until Gobrag fell asleep, but somehow he always awoke, croaking louder than before. Whatever they did, they could not escape his noisy presence.

"Something has to be done," said one of the frogs, finally. "We can't carry on with our singing anymore. We'll have to look for somewhere else to live."

The other frogs gasped in horror. They loved their garden with its beautiful, brightly colored flowers and its many fragrant plants, and most of all, their friends who lived there with them. But what could they do?

So the frogs agreed they had to look for a new home. Three of the older frogs volunteered to go on the search. Off they went, hopping out of the garden and into the big, wide world.

The trio hopped through the tall grass next to the rice field, over the ditch at its side, and across a temple yard until they arrived at the bank of a muddy stream. The stream seemed like a perfect spot, so they all jumped into the water to cool their hot little bodies.

After frolicking in the water for what seemed like hours, the frogs clambered onto a small island in the middle of the stream and sat in the sun expressing their pleasure in a chorus of croaks until they were quite hoarse.

Just as they were about to fall asleep, the island beneath them suddenly moved. It rose up in the air and they fell higgledy-piggledy into the water. Great waves and swirling currents tumbled them this way and that. Diving deep, the frogs swam as fast as they could until they reached a patch of reeds in shallow water near the bank. Clinging to the stalks and to one another, the frogs, peeping out, shrank back in terror at what they saw before them.

The island upon which, until a moment before, they had been sitting and singing, was now transformed into a huge lumbering monster, the likes of which they had never seen before! The monster reared its huge head, its horns arched high against the sky. It stared towards them. A massive cloven hoof crashed down in their midst, and then another, and a big wave of water washed over them and swept them up onto the bank.

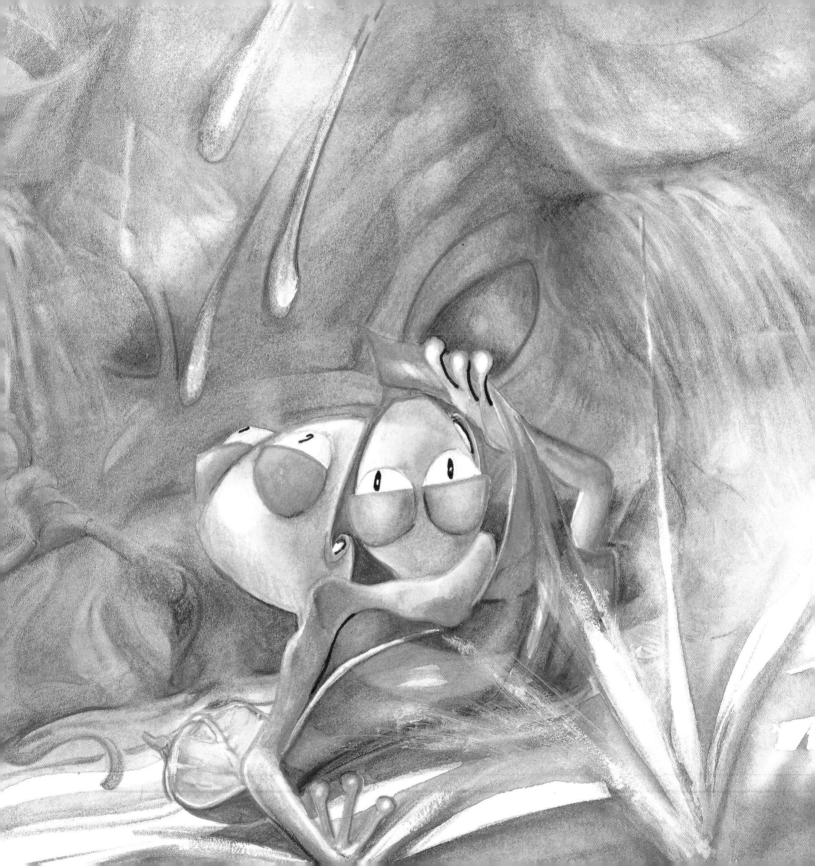

Reeling from fright, the frogs lost no time in leaping as quickly as they could from the dreadful place, and hurried back across the yard, over the ditch, through the tall grass, and finally through the gate to the relative peace of their garden home.

The other frogs were shocked to see how shaken and scared the trio were and asked anxiously what on earth had happened. As they started to tell their tale, everyone couldn't help but notice how Gobrag had edged closer to listen too.

"W-we m-m-met a m-m-m-monster," stammered one of the adventurers, at last.

"What do you mean, a monster?" exclaimed one of the others.

"A terrifying monster, bigger than anything we've ever seen. Bigger than a house, bigger than . . ."

Before he could finish, Gobrag boomed: "Bigger than me? Impossible! Don't you know that no beast is bigger than me?"

To prove his point, Gobrag puffed himself up, and cried:

"For as East is East and West is West,
I am the biggest and I am the best!"

He swallowed another huge gulp of air and pushed out his warty chest. "There—see what I mean!" he said, wobbling before them.

But the frogs knew that Gobrag was not the biggest thing on earth—the monster they had seen was a hundred times larger!

"Why, that monster out there was much meaner than you," said one of the little frogs. "He was the meanest thing I have ever seen."

"Nonsense!" roared Gobrag, "don't you know that no beast is meaner than I . . .

For as East is East and West is West,

I am the biggest and I am the best!"

And he blew himself up again, twice as big.

"That's not true," shrilled the frogs. "That monster was far uglier than you."

This was too much for Gobrag. "No beast is uglier than I!

For as East is East and West is West,

I am the biggest and I am the best!" he screamed, and, puffing himself up again, he ballooned out as big as a barrel.

"Bah!" barked the frogs in unison, "That monster was far scarier than you."

"Absolute rubbish!" bellowed Gobrag, who was by now thoroughly furious and as huge as a house! He took another stupendous gulp.

"As East is East and West is West . . ." he began, and then he got bigger and bigger and bigger . . . and bigger until, suddenly—he burst!

"Oh dear," said one of the frogs. "Poor old haughty toad. I really think he got a bit too big this time."

And then there was silence in the garden.

The frogs returned to their lily pads and sang tunefully, and peace reigned once again beneath the frangipani trees, though they couldn't help thinking that they really quite missed old Gobrag, the silly old toad.

The Saintly Stork

At the top of a very tall tamarind tree, far above a quiet Balinese village, there once lived a great white stork named Bebaka. From his huge untidy nest of twigs and leaves, he could look down on the nests of the all other birds, across the rice fields, and over the houses of the people.

And so he sat one morning, surveying his domain, his long yellow beak clattering and his head shaking gently from side to side.

It had been a good year in the village with plenty of rain. The paddy fields were alive with eels, crabs, frogs and fishes. The only problem was that so much food meant there were too many storks.

The flock had become so large that there were arguments over food every day.

Why, only yesterday some young upstart had the nerve to pinch a fat fish from Bebaka's very beak. He certainly wasn't getting the respect he deserved and he was determined to do something about it.

As he sat thinking about his unhappiness, Bebaka looked down at the temple below. A festival was in progress.

A brightly dressed group of people made their way into the inner courtyard. They placed their towering offerings, made out of fruit, flowers and multi-colored rice cakes, on a large platform and then kneeled to pray.

Overseeing the ceremony was the high priest, the Pedanda. Dressed in fine white robes and hat, his jewelled fingers held a silver prayer bell which tinkled gaily as he chanted his holy prayers. It was clear that he ruled the roost in the village.

Later that day, when the ceremony was over and everyone had filed out, the priest took his daily walk past the river. As he passed one of the deep pools, he rang his silver bell.

Bebaka nearly fell off his perch when he saw what happened next. Five of the fattest carp he had ever seen emerged to pay their respects to the priest. And what was more, they were accompanied by a very large and juicy-looking mud crab. The priest chatted to the creatures, threw them some rice and went on his way.

As Bebaka watched, he thought of a cunning plan. He would become Pedanda Bebaka—the holy bird—the master of all God's creatures! He would be a supremely wise old bird who would, finally, command the respect that he deserved.

Bebaka felt much better. He also felt rather hungry.

It wasn't long before he had gathered what he needed to look like a saintly stork. Round his ankles were two gold rings set with blood-red rubies. Round his shoulders draped a rich red cape. Around his neck strung a necklace of holy beads and on his head sat a felt hat adorned with flowers of beaten gold topped by a sparkling diamond. After an age of preening and admiring his reflection in a nearby pond, Bebaka set off in the direction of the river.

Arriving at the same deep pools where he had seen the priest, Bebaka stood on the riverbank on one leg and jangled his prayer bell. He was by now quite famished.

Soon enough several fat fish and the meaty mud crab appeared. A little startled to see the stork rather than the priest, they gaped in awe at Bebaka as he intoned a prayer and gave his blessing.

The mud crab spoke first. "What are you doing here?" he asked the bird. "Has the Pedanda sent you? What do you want from us?"

Bebaka rolled his head and replied: "I have been sent here to warn you that you are in very grave danger. Men with large poles and nets are on their way, as we speak, to catch you and take you home for their tea."

"Oh no!" cried the carp. "Whatever shall we do? We have heard stories about these men and their fishing rods. How can we escape?"

"Don't be afraid," answered Bebaka. "I am here to save you. I will myself take you out of this pool to safer waters. Just jump into my mouth and I will fly you to a place where you will never have to be afraid again."

The mud crab looked doubtful, but the fish were so scared they were ready to believe the holy bird.

As Bebaka opened his mouth, the first of the fish jumped into his lower beak. Bebaka gently closed his mouth and flew off. Their flight was very short because, as soon as they were out of sight of the others, Bebaka flew down to a large rock and prepared to enjoy his meal.

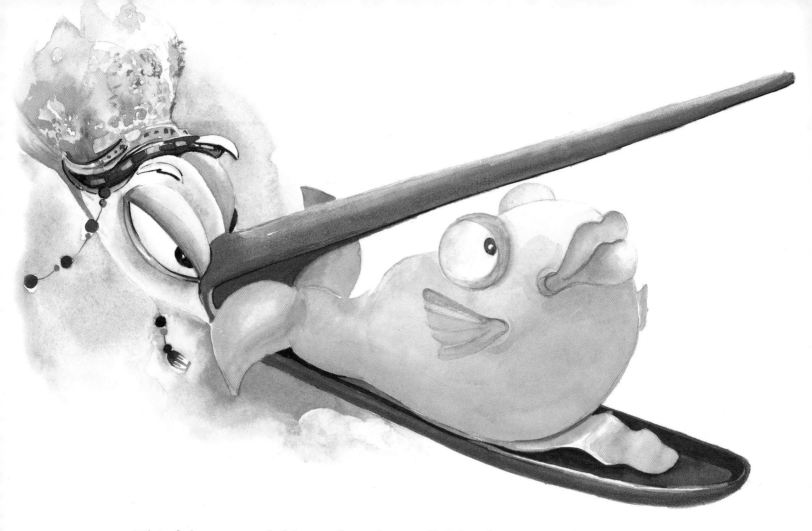

This fish was much bigger than the small fishes he was used to scooping up in his large beak in the paddy and it took him rather a long time to swallow the fat carp whole. As the fish went down his gullet it wriggled and twisted but soon enough it was safely in Bebaka's stomach. Bebaka burped loudly with appreciation and spat out the bony remains of the fish. He left these bones on the rock below.

Then he flew back to the deep pool and repeated the journey with the second carp, who soon found out to his horror that Bebaka was not a holy stork at all.

In no time, Bebaka had gobbled five fish and left their bones on the rock. He was very full indeed. But being a greedy bird, and believing he still had room for one more tasty morsel, he flew over to the pool and found the juicy mud crab.

"Where exactly have you taken those fishes?" asked the crab who was a rather suspicious fellow.

"Oh, I have taken them out of harm's way," said Bebaka, "to a place where no one will make a meal of them."

"But you weren't gone very long," argued the crab. "How do I know I will be safe from these fishermen you speak of?"

"I am a holy stork," answered Bebaka. "I am all-seeing and all-knowing, so I guarantee if you come with me you will never encounter the fisherman's net."

The crab studied Bebaka's holy garb a moment longer, then decided to put aside his fears and go along with him.

As Bebaka opened his mouth, the crab jumped in and the pair took off. As they flew, the crab peered out with his swivelling eyes to watch where they were going.

When Bebaka landed on his rock once more, the crab's eyes nearly fell out in shock. He had spied the pile of fish bones and realized to his horror that Bebaka was not a saint at all, but just a greedy bird who had eaten his friends.

Bebaka tried to swallow the crab as he had the other fish, but that wasn't a very smart thing to do. The crab, with its hard shell and strong pincers, didn't go down well at all. He started a merry dance in Bebaka's throat, and then clamped as hard as he could on the bird's gullet. Bebaka started to choke. He coughed and coughed, but the crab hung on with all his might. Bebaka shook his head from side to side, trying to fling the creature from his mouth. But still the crab held on.

Finally Bebaka collapsed in a heap next to the bones of his fishy victims.
The crab quickly crawled out and buried himself in a hole in the riverbank. "What a lucky escape!" he thought to himself.

Bebaka miraculously began to breathe again. After a little while, the crab stuck his head out of the hole and asked the stork, who was still lying on the ground: "Are you alive?"
"Only just," replied Bebaka softly.
"Let this be a lesson to you," said the crab. "You lied to us. You pretended to be a holy bird when you were nothing of the kind."

"I am sorry," said Bebaka, full of remorse. His brush with death had made him realize how precious life was. He was also ashamed of his trickery.
Slowly he dragged himself up and, head bowed in shame, he took off his priest's clothes and discarded his bell. Once he had regained his strength, he flew home to his nest and decided that, from then on, he would be the holiest of holy birds. He wouldn't tell any more lies and he would share whatever he had with anyone who came along.

The Golden Axe

In a little hut on the fringes of a forest there once lived a poor woodcutter named Lentjod. He was a kind old man who lived with his wife and made his living from chopping firewood which he sold in a nearby village.

Lentjod enjoyed his work, though it had not made him rich. He barely earned enough money to pay for food for himself and his wife. His six children, now grown up, had gone to work in the village. Lentjod missed them all but there was nothing he could do. He wanted to build a big house for everyone to live in together but he just didn't have enough money.

One particularly fine spring morning, Lentjod was outside as usual, cutting wood by the side of a deep gorge that dropped towards a raging river. *Chop, chop, chop,* went his axe as he cut a fallen tree trunk into equal pieces.

Then Lentjod swung too hard and his axe flew from his hands. He watched in horror as it went tumbling down the gully, bouncing over rocks and moss until it hit the water with a loud splash.

"Oh no!" he cried. "My axe!"

Without his axe, Lentjod would not be able to work and he certainly couldn't afford to buy a new one. He would have to climb down the gully and try to find it. Slowly and carefully he clambered down the steep slope, wheezing as he went —for Lentjod was not a young man any more.

Finally he reached the water's edge, but he could not see his axe beneath the swirling currents, hard as he peered. He walked up and down the river's edge and kept searching, but there was no sign of it.

Just as he was about to give up and go home, he was startled by the sight of a young woman bathing in a shallow rock pool by the raging river. She was the most beautiful girl he had ever seen.

He had no way of knowing, of course, that this was not an ordinary girl. In fact, she was a *dedari*—a Balinese fairy—who had come down to earth from heaven, to bathe. Not wishing to intrude, Lentjod turned to leave. But it was too late; she had seen him.

"Wait," she commanded. As Lentjod turned, she asked gently: "What troubles you, old man? I can see that you have lost something that is of great value to you."

Her voice was as soft and magical as the tinkle of a silver bell.

Lentjod was spellbound and started telling her about his loss and how he would not be able to make a living without the tool of his trade.

She looked at him warmly and, smiling, pulled from the water a gleaming axe made from burnished steel.

"Is this the axe you seek?" she asked the old man. Lentjod looked at the shining metal axe.

"Oh, if only it were," he cried.

"Please take it," said the *dedari*, "for I found it in the place where yours was lost."

"Oh, fair maiden," Lentjod said solemnly, "it is not mine to take. However much I would love to own this axe, my conscience will not allow me to claim it as my own."

"Very well," said the spirit, looking at him long and hard.

Then, again smiling enchantingly, she pulled out from the water another axe, this time, one made of solid silver.

"Is this the axe you seek?" she asked the old man. Lentjod looked at the blade glinting in the sun. Why, with that axe, he would become a wealthy man indeed.

"Oh, if only it were," he cried. "But I cannot accept it, for it is not mine."

The *dedari* was quiet as she now retrieved an axe of solid gold from the water. Lentjod could hardly believe his eyes.

"Is this your axe?" she again asked the old man.

Lentjod stared longingly at the beautiful metal. The head of the axe alone was worth more than Lentjod would earn in his lifetime. He thought of all he would be able to do if he had such an axe, but, being an honest fellow, he said: "I wish, fair maiden, that it were mine. But it is not."

The *dedari* shrugged sadly and sighed: "Well, old man, there is nothing more to do. Your axe seems well and truly lost."

Lentjod bowed his head, feeling tired and defeated. He looked up at the top of the hill to where he must climb. He turned back to the maiden to wish her goodbye, but she had disappeared.

With a heavy heart he slowly started up the steep gorge. He dragged his old, weary body up the slope, his head pounding in the midday heat. When he finally reached the top, he was faint with exhaustion.

After a short rest, he continued home to his simple hut. As he approached, his wife came running out. "Lentjod! Lentjod!" she cried.

"What is it? What's happened?" he asked worriedly. After what had just happened, he couldn't bear to hear any more bad news.

His wife could hardly speak; she seemed so shaken. "There was a girl, a beautiful girl . . . " she started.

Lentjod took her gently by the arm and sat her down. When she had caught her breath, he asked her to explain.

The words came tumbling out: "A beautiful maiden came to visit me and told me that you were the most humble and honest man she had ever met. She left a present for you."

Lentjod's wife then led Lentjod to their hut. A large package, wrapped in the finest silk, lay on the kitchen table.

Lentjod quickly unwrapped the parcel and gazed in amazement at the most extraordinary object he had ever seen: an axe with a blade of finest gold, and a handle fashioned from silver and studded with diamonds, rubies and emeralds.

Lentjod's mouth fell open in astonishment.

"That was no ordinary maiden, she must have been a *dedari*!" he gasped.

The old couple smiled at each other as they realized their good fortune. They would sell the axe and Lentjod would never have to work again. He would build a grand house in the village and the whole family would be together once again.

And Lentjod would spend many a sunny day with a grandchild on his knee telling the story of the *dedari* and how it always pays to be honest.

The Talkative Turtle

During a time of terrible drought in the land, when there had been no rain for months and all the rivers and the lakes had turned to dust, a dejected little turtle sat crying softly to himself by a dry and barren creek.

"Oh my," he sobbed. "What is to become of me? I am all alone here, where there is not a drop of water to drink."

Poor Empas—for that was his name —was a shadow of his former self. Why, he had once been one of the most talkative turtles around.

In fact, he used to talk so much at school that he was always getting into trouble. His teacher would become very annoyed with his non-stop chatter and make him stand outside the classroom so that she could conduct her lessons in peace.

And his mother, father and siblings had grown so tired of his talkative nature that they ignored him completely when he spoke.

Empas had lost them all during the terrible drought, probably because he had been so busy talking he hadn't paid attention when his family were discussing their plans to move to a better place. If only his family were with him now, he thought, he would be quiet and listen attentively to everything they had to say.

But it was all too late now.

Suddenly Empas heard a commotion on the other bank—a great swirling of dust and the beating of wings. There stood two large white geese who, despite looking a little travel weary, were busily preening their feathers and honking loudly.

The poor little turtle summoned his energy and cried: "Help! Help m . . eeee!'

The geese heard Empas' plaintive cry and, stretching their long necks and thrusting their yellow beaks towards him, they hissed (as geese do): "What is it? Whatever is the matter?"

Sobbing convulsively, Empas started telling his pitiful tale, and, despite his earlier promise not to talk too much, he stammered away: "Please help me, I am in a terrible mess, the water's all gone, there's nothing to eat, nothing to drink, what's to become of me, oh dear, oh dear, oh dear. Please help me . . . please . . . there's a drought, the water's all dried up . . . I've lost my family, I don't know what to do . . ."

"All right, all right," interrupted the geese, quickly realizing that Empas would have sat there all day telling his tale.

They, too, knew about the drought and were themselves on an urgent journey to find water. They had to make haste.

Fortunately for Empas, these geese were kind creatures who decided to help him. But how would they get him away from this barren place? While they could fly away at speed, poor Empas could only crawl along on the ground. And we all know how slowly turtles move, out of water.

They all thought long and hard of a plan.

Then one goose said excitedly: "I've got it! Wait here." And he rushed off into a bush.

Moments later he returned with a long and sturdy stick in his beak.

"Now listen here," he instructed Empas. "My friend and I will each carry one end of the stick in our beaks. You will clamp your jaws tightly on the middle. This way we can fly over this dry and dusty land and transport you to somewhere more lush and welcoming."

Empas began to speak: "Oh, how can I ever thank you, you are two of the kindest geese I have ever met. I wish I could introduce you to my family. They would . . ."

One of the geese interrupted him again. "Look, this plan of ours will work only if you don't talk. For as soon as you open your mouth you will fall from the stick to the hard ground below. Is that clear?"

Empas nodded and realized that for the first time in his life he really had to keep his mouth shut.

The three companions took the piece of wood firmly in their mouths. The geese then started to run, their wings flapping madly as they tried to take off. It was not an easy task, but soon the three of them were airborne, although they had to fly very low.

Now as you can imagine, the sight of two geese flying with a long stick from which a turtle was suspended caused much excitement as they passed over the creatures below. And, of course, everyone was curious about the story behind this odd trio.

First of all they passed some herons, perched high up in a tree.

"My, oh my, what a strange sight," exclaimed one heron. "Pray tell us, little turtle, how did you come to be suspended between two geese?"

Empas was about to answer with a long and involved story of his adventure when he suddenly remembered that he could not—must not—speak. So he said nothing as they flew on, leaving the herons thinking him very rude indeed.

Then they passed some monkeys who were sitting beside the road waiting for tourists to feed them some nuts.

"What a sight," they said. "What's a small turtle like you doing hanging around with geese like that?"

Empas was keen to tell them his tale, but, once again, he remembered that he opened his mouth at his peril. Again they flew past with him saying nothing. The monkeys thought him a very strange fellow indeed.

A little later on, the daring trio passed a slinking, scabby dog who looked at them with something more than wonder. This scrawny fellow had food on his mind. He knew how ferocious geese could be when provoked, so he set his heart—or rather his stomach—on the tasty turtle.

Being a cunning fellow, he realized all he had to do was get Empas to loosen his grip on the stick. As he trailed the three travellers, he began to think about how to make the turtle open his mouth and fall to the ground.

"Oh my, you must be very tired," he shouted up to Empas. And he gave an enormous yawn.

Poor little Empas was certainly feeling a little weary and wanted to yawn too. But he knew he must not open his mouth. Thus, despite the overwhelming urge, he managed to keep his jaws shut.

"Oh my, what a sight," shouted the dog again. "I have never seen anything so funny in all my life!" And he rolled over and started to laugh heartily.

As the dog's laughter became louder and more raucous, Empas could feel the start of a giggle welling up inside him, but he struggled valiantly to keep from laughing out loud. To distract himself, he turned his thoughts to his family, and his sadness immediately stopped him from laughing.

The dog began to lose patience.

"You, turtle, are the most ridiculous creature I have ever seen," he yelled. "Just look at you hanging there between those two ganders."

Empas wanted so much to retort, but instead he gathered all the will power he could muster and clung on resolutely to the stick. The dog continued running below the trio, not giving up.

"You, turtle, are the ugliest creature I have ever seen. Just look at your scaly legs and arms, and beady eyes."

Empas felt very hurt and angry, but still he refused to succumb.

"You, turtle, are the saddest creature I have ever seen," barked the dog. "Why, even your family must think so, for they left you behind!"

This was the last straw. Empas was so angry by the insult that he could contain himself no longer.

"Oh no, they didn't!" he replied indignantly, and then felt himself drop quickly to the ground below.

Having tucked himself inside his shell as he fell, Empas felt himself bounce along on the ground before coming to a stop on a mossy bank.

He stayed tucked inside as he felt the snout of the dog sniff around him. He was very scared.

"Oh, if only I had kept quiet," he thought.

All of a sudden he heard a loud noise. It was the geese who had followed after him. With a great flapping of wings they landed right beside Empas and dropped the stick in front of his shell.

"*Honk! Honk! Honk!*" they went as they moved forward together, their strong yellow beaks snapping at the dog.

The dog knew immediately that he was no match for these two powerful birds— and regretfully slunk off into the bushes.

Empas emerged, timidly, from his shell.

The two geese glared at him, saying: "Have you learned your lesson yet? You've got one last chance. Grab the stick once again and we'll be off. But remember, think before you speak. You may not be so lucky next time!"

Empas acquiesced and his friends took off once more. This time he did not talk at all. At long last, they arrived at a small pond and the geese let Empas down gently before going on their way.

A most extraordinary thing happened next. Empas was wondering what to do when he heard his name being called: "Empas, Empas! Where have you been?"

Empas was so happy; it was his mother's voice! And, as luck would have it, she was with the rest of his family.

Empas yearned to tell them all about his adventure, but he had learnt an important lesson from his ordeal. He now knew when to talk, and when to keep his mouth shut. So he sat quietly and listened instead to their tale.

The Rajah who Lost his Head

In a large palace, surrounded by beautiful gardens and a moat, there once lived a young rajah who was very spoiled. He had a whole team of servants and courtiers to attend to his every need. The noblemen would seek out the prince to try and become his friend. The ordinary people in the village came regularly to the palace to pay their respects to the rajah and his royal family.

But the prince had no interest in any of them. He had only one friend with whom he wanted to spend his time—and that was Lutung, his pet monkey.

Now Lutung was no ordinary monkey. He was a very clever fellow indeed. He could perform the most amazing tricks for his royal companion.

He could juggle ten mangoes at once. He could climb the curtains, swing from the rafters and do somersaults in the air. He could dance, sing and play the fool. But he would perform only for the rajah—no one else could make him do a thing.

Every evening, the young rajah would sit down to dinner with Lutung, who would be dressed in the finest clothes and seated in his little golden chair. After their meal, Lutung would entertain his master with his tricks until tears of laughter rolled down the rajah's cheeks.

The room would end up in a terrible mess but there was always someone to clean up after them. After the performance, the pair would go hand-in-hand to bed.

Many in the palace began to worry that the rajah loved his monkey too much. Why didn't he want any human friends? Some people were even jealous of Lutung's place in his master's heart.

When the rajah was old enough, his ministers decided that he should get married. They thought a wife might bring him to his senses.

The rajah didn't want a wife. But his ministers said that if he didn't comply, they would be forced to take Lutung away, so he had no choice in the matter.

The ministers searched the kingdom high and low until they found a beautiful young girl from a noble family. They made arrangements to meet the girl's father, and went to visit him wearing their finest silk sarongs. Tucked in each minister's sarong was a jewelled dagger with a wavy blade called a *kris*.

They brought ceremonial gifts of clothes, food and a ring. They talked about the virtues of the young rajah. And to further convince the girl's father of the advantages of the union, they presented him with a small fortune.

Eventually, everyone came to an agreement. The wedding date was set and preparations for the ceremony began. It was to be a very grand wedding indeed.

When the big day arrived, the palace began to fill with impressive noblemen and women dressed in their finest clothes accompanied by their attendants carrying presents.

Three large open-sided grass-roofed structures called *balés* had been constructed for the wedding. One was for the ceremony, another for the banquet and a third for the entertainment.

Inside the *balés* were elaborate offerings to the gods including great pyramids of fruit, flowers and roast chickens, as well as dainty little figures cut out from palm leaf. There were tables and chairs for the important guests and Balinese noblemen. And all the common people from the surrounding villages crowded around outside.

Before long the rajah and his bride appeared. A murmur of appreciation arose from the crowd as they saw the couple's fine wedding clothes and beautiful gold jewelry.

The priest performed the wedding ceremony which, to the rajah, seemed to last forever. He sulked throughout, thinking only of his dear Lutung.

At the wedding dinner, the rajah sat in sullen silence. The silver platters carrying the roast suckling pig and other spicy dishes could not tempt him. Where was his darling monkey? Surely he would be allowed to entertain him on his wedding day?

Sadly, the ministers had locked Lutung up in a small room in the palace. They had even tied him to a chair to be doubly sure he would not disrupt the wedding party. But it didn't take Lutung long to gnaw through the string and free himself. He hid behind the door waiting to escape when someone came in with his dinner.

Meanwhile, the young rajah was getting very restless. His beautiful bride was of no interest to him. And all the rich and noble people bored him to tears.

"Oh, where is my dearest Lutung?" he thought to himself. "He is the only one in the whole world who can make me laugh."

Soon the party was shown into the *balé* for the evening's entertainment. The ministers hoped the spoiled rajah would at last show some interest in what they had arranged. First to arrive were two storytellers, who began telling the ancient tales of Bali. While the audience sat spellbound, the rajah only sulked.

"I want Lutung!" he cried, "not these two fools."

Then came three beautiful little girls who performed the finest Balinese dance called the *legong*. Dressed from head to foot in silk cloth, their heads adorned with quivering gold head-dresses and frangipani blossoms, the three dancers amazed the audience as they moved elegantly to the music of the traditional Balinese orchestra called a *gamelan*.

Only one member of the audience was not impressed.

"This is boring," complained the rajah. "Where is Lutung?"

The prince could stand it no longer. He made his excuses, saying he had a terrible headache, and went into his private garden for some peace and quiet. His new wife waited as he left and then followed twenty paces behind him.

The rajah came to a large wooden bed under a scented frangipani tree and lay down. Suddenly he felt a tug at his silk sarong. He looked down and was overjoyed to see his own dear Lutung.

But the rajah was so tired after the day's celebrations that he didn't want to play any games or watch Lutung perform any tricks. He lay on his pillows, closed his eyes and told Lutung to make sure no one disturbed him.

Lutung obediently took his place next to the rajah.

Before long the worried bride approached to see what the matter was. Lutung, remembering what he had been told, jumped at her and bared his fangs.

She was scared away in an instant.

A senior minister came next. He wanted the rajah to return to the wedding. But no sooner had he appeared than Lutung grabbed his legs. Frightened by the ferocious monkey, he quickly ran away.

As the rajah continued resting, Lutung sat guard beside him.

After a while, a huge bluebottle flew near the rajah's head. As the fly buzzed around, Lutung removed the *kris* from the rajah's sarong, ready to chop it into pieces.

"*Buzz! Buzz! Buzz!*" went the fly as Lutung observed it warily.

Suddenly the fly landed on the rajah's neck and Lutung brought the *kris* down heavily, killing the fly. But unfortunately, the monkey also chopped off the rajah's head.

Lutung looked down in horror. His master was dead. He ran far away from the palace and was never seen again.

The tale of the rajah who lost his head was told far and wide as a warning to those who believed they could make pets out of wild animals. It is far better for everyone—both animal and man—if the animals are left where they belong . . . in the wild.

The Ant and the Dove

Once upon a time, in a paddy field in Bali, there lived a pretty little dove called Kunan. He had a steely blue-grey cap, a shiny green neck and bright orange eyes. Kunan spent his days flying over the streams and through the trees, cooing gaily in the sun. His favorite food was the rice that grew in the paddies. He would fly down and perch on the stalks while he pecked at the small grains.

Until, that is, the farmer's son saw him. Then the rice field would echo with a loud "*clack! clack! clack!*" as the boy—sitting in a small bamboo hut built above the ground —shook his clacker from morning to night to frighten the birds away.

This was an important job. The Balinese believe that rice is a gift from the gods, and it is eaten with every meal. While it is growing in the fields the Balinese perform many small ceremonies to make sure it grows big and tasty. They also make sure that the doves, weavers and other birds don't eat it before the harvest.

Early one sunny morning, Kunan had again eaten a fine breakfast before the farmer's son arrived to shoo him away. He flew into the trees by the stream to rest, feeling full and happy.

But all of a sudden, he saw something very small struggling in the water below. Kunan flew down to the bank for a closer look.

There was a small ant going round and round in the water. The water was moving very fast and the poor little creature was drowning.

Kunan had to act quickly. He grabbed a blade of grass and, perched on the side of the bank, held it out to the ant. The creature managed to grab the grass and Kunan pulled him, coughing and spluttering, to safety.

It was a warm day and the ant dried quickly in the sun.

"How can I ever thank you?" said the ant to Kunan. "You saved my life!"

"It was nothing," replied Kunan modestly. "I would have done the same for anyone else in trouble."

"Well, if there is anything I can do for you in return, please let me know," said the ant.

"Of course I will," replied Kunan, although he thought it very unlikely that such a small creature would be able to help him, who was so much bigger.

Soon the two friends parted. Kunan flew back to the tree and the ant crawled back into the bushes.

Before long it was midday and Kunan thought about lunch. He flew off to the paddy fields again. But the farmer's boy was there.

As Kunan came nearer, he realized he had been spotted. But instead of making his usual "*clack! clack! clack!*" the boy rushed away.

Kunan thought this a little strange, but couldn't believe his luck. He went down to the field and stuffed himself with rice.

After he had eaten his fill, he flew off to a large Banyan tree nearby. Perched on one of the branches, he tucked his shiny head under his wing and was soon fast asleep.

What Kunan didn't know was that the boy was not very far away at all. He had crept to the edge of the field and hidden himself from the bird. He was waiting to see where the dove went for his afternoon nap.

He now slowly crawled among the rice plants to where Kunan slept, carrying a bamboo blowpipe and some poisoned darts. When he was under the tree, he stood up, put the pipe to his mouth, puffed out his cheeks and took aim.

Poor Kunan still had no idea of the danger he was in.

But luck was on his side that sunny afternoon. The same ant that Kunan had rescued was nearby. He saw the danger the bird was in, and knew he had to act quickly to save his friend.

He summoned his fellow ants and together they crawled up the farmer boy's bare legs. At the very moment when the boy was about to release the dart, they bit him as hard as they could.

"*Yeeoww!*" cried the boy very loudly. Kunan woke up with a start, flying high in the air. The dart missed him by a mile and the blowpipe fell to the ground. The boy frantically brushed the ants from his legs and ran screaming back to his shelter.

Kunan flew down to the ants. "Thank you for saving my life," he said gratefully.

"You are very welcome," his small friend replied. "Like I always say, one good deed deserves another."

Kunan smiled, thanked his friend again, and then flew back to the trees where he cooed a beautiful song for all the ants of the forest.

The Dog who Flattered a Crow

In a village in Bali there once lived a very skinny, very cunning dog. He was skinny because he never had enough to eat. But luckily he was cunning, because he had to keep his wits about him in order to scavenge for food.

He lived with a Balinese family who kept the dog to protect them. At night he would bark and wail to frighten the witches and evil spirits away. The other dogs in the village did the same. Surprisingly enough the villagers always managed to sleep through this din.

Although the dog lived with the family, food was scarce and the dog was at the bottom of the list at mealtimes. He would sit as close as he dared to the table when the family ate their dinner, hoping for a few scraps to fall his way, but the pickings were always lean.

He would follow the women of the house as they placed their daily offerings to the gods around the compound. These food offerings, usually some rice on small squares of banana leaf, provided the dog with a few mouthfuls, but they were hardly enough to make him fat.

The dog's favorite times were when the family held large ceremonies and the house would teem with guests and the tables would be full of good things to eat. Often, pieces of delicious cooked food would fall to the floor and the dog would be ready to snap them up.

Sadly, there had not been a holy day or a feast of any kind for quite some time, so the dog was very hungry indeed.

As there was so little to eat at home, the dog decided to try further afield. He slunk off through the back garden, across the stream and into a small wood.

All of a sudden his nose started to twitch. "What a wonderful smell," he thought to himself. "If I'm not mistaken, that is the aroma of roast meat."

He put his nose to the ground and tried to sniff out the smell. It wasn't in the grass. It wasn't at the base of the tree either. Where could it possibly be?

He lifted his nose in the air and sniffed again. Then his attention was drawn to the loud flapping of wings above him. A glossy king crow had just lighted on a tree, and in his beak was a large juicy piece of roast pork.

The dog's mouth watered. He so badly wanted that tasty treat. But how could he get it from the crow? He couldn't climb; neither could he fly.

Then the cunning dog had an idea.

He looked up at the crow and exclaimed: "What a gorgeous bird! What beautiful shiny green feathers. Such a delicate purple sheen!"

The king crow quivered with delight at the dog's compliments.

"You are the most handsome bird I have ever seen," continued the dog. "Your bright yellow beak shines like the sun. Your eyes sparkle like the stars."

The crow immediately puffed up proudly and delightedly. He had never heard such flattery.

His beady eyes letting neither the crow nor the meat out of his sight, the dog continued: "I wonder if your voice matches your beauty. Why, then you would surely be King of the birds. No other creature could compare to you if your sweet bird song matched your exquisite appearance!"

At this, the vain crow couldn't resist the chance to show off. It was simply too much for him.

He opened his mouth wide and began to caw loudly. As he did so, the fat piece of meat fell from his beak towards the ground.

The sly dog was ready and waiting. He ran forward, opened his mouth and caught the tasty morsel in his open jaws. He swallowed it up in an instant, then licked his lips with immense satisfaction.

"Delicious!" he said, feeling very pleased with himself as the crow squawked angrily above him.

"Indeed you have a keen voice," the dog now taunted. "It's only a pity you haven't got a brain to match!"

And with that, he slunk back home.

The poor crow. If he had been smarter, he would never have trusted the flattering words of a cunning dog.

A Tale of Two Sisters

In a little village in Bali, there lived two sisters named Bawang and Suna. Suna was the elder sibling and jealous of Bawang. Both were very beautiful, but while Bawang's beauty came from within, Suna's was only skin deep. Bawang worked hard and Suna was lazy. While Bawang was modest, Suna was vain. And whereas Bawang always spoke the truth, Suna told only lies.

There was much to do in the family compound. Theirs was a large family, with father, brothers, sisters, infants, aunties and uncles all living under one roof. Their mother was busy with buying food at the market and looking after everyone's needs. So the two girls had to do all the household chores.

If there was not water to be fetched or meals to be cooked, there were floors to be swept, pots to be cleaned, animals to be fed, clothes to be washed, linen to be mended—a non-stop grind from sunrise to sunset.

Although the two girls were both responsible for all these tasks, the work was never fairly divided. Suna left all the difficult tasks to Bawang while she herself pretended to be busy—either making dainty offerings for the temple or sprinkling herbs into the cooking pot or sewing a new blouse, most probably for herself. If truth be known, Bawang did almost everything.

For example, if there was a tedious chore, like threshing the rice or cleaning out the pig-pen, Suna would tell Bawang: "You do it this time, dear sister; it will be my turn next." Or she would say: "I am busy at the moment, I will help you later."

But of course, Suna's turn never came, or whatever she was doing was never finished before her sister had done the job all by herself.

Sometimes Suna would appear just before Bawang had finished her work. Pretending to be concerned she would say: "Oh my poor dear, have you really had to do all this on your own? I am so sorry but I have been so busy elsewhere. Now don't do another thing. Run along. Take a rest and a nice cool bath in the river."

Gratefully, Bawang would thank Suna for being so thoughtful and gladly hurry away to the river. The sneaky Suna would then mess up her hair and crumple her clothes and spread a little dirt on her dress (after all, sweet Bawang would be doing the washing) before pretending to be working.

More often than not, this is the time when their mother would appear. Seeing Suna looking tired and unkempt, she imagined her to have worked long and hard all day without help from her sister.

When asked where Bawang was, Suna would reply: "I really don't know, mother. She hasn't been here, though I think she may have gone to the river to bathe." And her mother would become very upset, thinking Suna did all the work.

One day, there was a large festival in the village. It was a very important ceremony and, for weeks before the event, all the villagers had been busy preparing the temple for the great feast.

In the sisters' house, there was more to do than ever. As usual, the hardest work was left to the ever-willing Bawang while the selfish Suna spent all her time prettying herself and making a new lacy blouse and silk sarong for the grand occasion.

The duties grew so heavy that poor little Bawang could hardly cope any longer. Apart from the usual chores, there were offerings to be made, cake to be baked and thousands of strips of palm leaf to be cut and made into delicate baskets and figures and rosettes for the ceremony. Bawang was nearing the end of her strength. She was so tired that she could neither eat nor rest at night, and while the others lay soundly asleep, she would lie quietly on her bed of bamboo slats, tears running down her cheeks.

On the morning of the festival, the family compound was alive with bustle and excitement. Everyone was running around preparing for the occasion. Bawang, as always, rose before the others and went straight into the kitchen. She cut kindling and lit the fire, then put cakes on the griddle and water in the pot to boil.

Next she began feeding the animals—first, the geese, chickens and ducks in the yard, and the cow tethered in the garden. Then she prepared to feed the pigs at the back of the house. She began making her way to the pig sty with the heavy bucket of swill balanced on her head. But her head began to spin and she began to sway. Her knees buckled under her and she fell face down in the mud.

Meanwhile, in the kitchen, her mother was very cross. She had come in to see if breakfast was ready, only to find the pot dry, the fire out and the cakes turned to cinders. She shouted Bawang's name but there was no reply.

She then shouted for Suna who just a moment ago had woken up. With a broom in her hand, Suna put her head round the door.

"What's the matter, mother?" she asked sweetly.

"Where's Bawang?" her mother asked crossly.

"I have no idea," replied Suna, and seeing a chance to get off work, she offered to go and find her.

Her mother told her to go quickly, so Suna went off to the back of the compound where she thought her sister might be. She discovered Bawang lying lifeless in the mud. She was afraid—not because she was worried about her sister but because the truth about her own laziness might now be discovered.

She knelt beside Bawang, turned her over and reassured herself that she was indeed alive. She shook her sister none too gently and told her to get up on her feet. But still Bawang did not stir.

In frustration, the cruel girl took the bucket of swill and emptied it over her sister's head. This seemed to revive Bawang a little so that she could now raise her head. But she still could not stand.

Suna thought the only remedy was to take her to the river. It was not very far away, and she dragged her sister there. At the river's edge, she shoved Bawang into the water and returned home without looking back.

Looking quite dishevelled, for once with reason, Suna told her mother that she had found Bawang bathing in the river.

Now since she had fed all the animals, she asked if she be excused to prepare for the feast. She wanted to look her best. Her mother was furious—not with Suna, of course, but with Bawang.

Meanwhile, the fast-flowing water had revived Bawang. Coming to her senses, she realized she had to hurry home for the festival. Gathering up her skirt, she ran down the path to the house.

Mother was waiting at the gate, her sister close behind. Not even giving her a chance to explain, her mother shouted at her.

"You are a lazy, good-for-nothing child," she screamed. "Go to your room immediately! And stay there. You will not be coming to the feast, that's for sure."

Poor Bawang took to her bed and sobbed herself to sleep. When she awoke later and all the others had left for the temple, she decided she would run away, far from the constant toil and sorrow, where her family would not find her. Surely they wouldn't miss her, she thought, her tears brimming over once more. She fought them back; she would cry no more.

She went to the kitchen, drank a cup of water and ate some cake and a little rice. Bundling up a few clothes and some food for the journey, she looked around her one last time and, closing the door softly behind her, went out into the bright sunlight.

Before long, she arrived at the river's edge. She bathed in the soothing waters and then, after wading upstream, she climbed onto a large flat rock. Stretching out, she allowed herself to be dried and restored by the healing rays of the sun. Once again, she drifted off to sleep.

When she awoke, the sun was just setting and a cool evening breeze caressed her face. Soon it would be night, so she must push on. There was a small path leading along the water's edge and she decided to follow wherever it might lead.

Night came very soon, but a great silvery moon shone so brightly that everything in its path was clear. Bawang's journey became harder. The pathway led over huge boulders and under steep, fern-covered cliffs. Sometimes the path seemed to disappear altogether and Bawang would pause, trying to find some sign of it again. She thought about turning back, but realized she had nowhere to go back to.

When the full moon had moved directly above her, she rested wearily on a smooth rock shelf that overhung the racing waters of the river below. A flight of steps cut from the rock, dipping down sharply and out of sight. These steps must lead somewhere, she thought, as she carefully lowered herself over the edge and slowly felt her way downwards. The steps ended suddenly and she found herself on a wide ledge. A current of warm air seemed to come from a huge slab of rock in front of her.

It turned out to be a cave and, despite feeling a little afraid, Bawang entered. She stumbled blindly through a deep, dark passage. Its sides were smooth and even, and the ground was sandy underfoot.

Before long, she felt the tunnel slope upwards and she faced another set of steps, these leading upwards. As she began to climb, she saw a glimmer of light. Her heart pounding, she reached the last step and, for a moment, was blinded by a strong, silvery light. The moon shone once again and she stepped into its brightness.

Looking all around her she found herself in a wide glade carpeted with springy grass and enclosed on three sides by dense forest. To her right a small spring gurgled into a crystal clear pool. Bawang washed her face in the pool and quenched her thirst. The cool water was pure and refreshing—she had never tasted anything so perfect.

But she was still tired and very hungry. And she had to find shelter for the rest of the night.

At the edge of the glade she saw a large Banyan tree. Its gnarled and knotted trunk branched out into a web of twisted roots. The tree would provide perfect shelter. Bawang started gathering sticks and fern to make a bed. While doing so, she looked over a crumbling wall at the furthest roots, and saw beyond it the weathered thatch of a small pavilion. Bawang quickly realized that this was a holy place, a temple nestled under the sacred Banyan tree.

She hurried back to the pool and began preparing herself for worship in the temple. After a bath, she gathered some frangipani and hibiscus blossoms from nearby. Using several reeds, she quickly wove a small basket. Then she sprinkled water from the spring over the flowers, placing some in her hair and the rest in her basket. Last, she coiled a large banana leaf and filled it with the holy water. Now she was ready.

She walked through the glade and under the shadow of the giant tree to the temple of the wood. The mossy stones and crumbled walls gave the impression that no human had been here in years.

Nevertheless she sensed that she was not alone, and that the spirit of the place somehow lived on. There was a feeling of peace and happiness there, which was both reassuring and strange.

Bawang set the cup of holy water next to herself and the offerings of flowers on a rock near the shrine and there she knelt to pray. Once she was at peace with herself and the spirit, a wondrous thing happened. Out of the night all the creatures of the forest soundlessly emerged. There were snakes, monkeys, deer, squirrels, bats, beetles, wolves, toads, birds of prey—and even a solitary tiger. They quietly formed a great circle around the unsuspecting girl, now deep in prayer.

Bawang took a flower from her basket and, holding it aloft between her fingers, she prayed to the gods. She pressed it to her forehead and then placed it before the shrine. This she did three times. She turned to take the holy water but the cup was not there. She must have knocked it over. She reached behind her and then felt something touch her shoulder.

She spun round and found herself face to face with an old woman—the oldest, ugliest and most fearsome character she had ever seen. Bawang was terrified and clasped her hands over her face. The old woman's bony hands patted her shoulder reassuringly, and a cracked but gentle voice said: "Don't be afraid."

Bawang lowered her hands and looked into the old woman's eyes. What wise, kind eyes they were. She was frightened no more. The ancient hag smiled a toothless smile and asked Bawang to face the shrine once again. Then she moved forward and sprinkled the girl with the holy water three times.

When all was done, Bawang rose and thanked the old woman for her kindness. She was about to ask where she was when suddenly she noticed all the animals assembled nearby.

She jumped back in fright but the woman just cackled loudly and said: "These animals are all friends, they will not harm you."

Then, with a strange throaty roar, she waved her arm and the animals filed out into the forest. She took Bawang's arm and led her back through the temple, through the wood to a small clearing in which was a simple hut with a thatched roof. Once inside, the old lady gave Bawang some rice porridge from a large pot. With grateful tears in her eyes, Bawang thanked and hugged her. The woman merely nodded and, before disappearing into the night, showed Bawang to a bed of straw in the corner. Bawang stretched out on her makeshift bed and immediately fell asleep.

When she awoke the sun was already high in the sky. She opened the shutters of the window over her bed and sunlight flooded in. A balmy breeze sent sparks flickering in the grate. She could smell the porridge simmering on the stove but, although she was hungry, she felt it would be wrong to serve herself without the old lady's permission. She peered out of the window and saw a beautiful garden full of flowers and fruit trees.

Feeling refreshed and free she began to sing, something she had not done for a very long time.

As she sang, a brilliant golden-yellow bird flew out of the forest on to the branch of a mango tree. He trilled loudly as if in answer:

> "Tra-la-la, tra-la-tring
> A song I shall sing
> And for you fair maid
> A gift I shall bring."

Its song was as golden as the sheen on its plumes. Never had Bawang heard such a divine sound. She wished it would last forever, but the bird finished its song and flew off back to the wood.

A few minutes later, the old woman came back to the hut looking more hunched, frail and wrinkled than ever. Bawang happily embraced her and said that she had slept well. The woman then placed some cakes, fruit and porridge on the table and Bawang ate till she was full. She then helped clean up everything.

The old lady told her she had to go away for a few days. She asked Bawang to care for the animals and said: "Please help yourself to anything in the garden." Then, without another word, she hobbled out of the hut and was gone.

Bawang was sad to see the old lady go. She had become very fond of her during their short time together, and she realized this was no ordinary person. But Bawang was now the happiest she had ever been in her life.

Not an idle girl by nature, she set to work cleaning the house from top to bottom, feeding the animals and tending the garden. When she was finished she went to the brook to bathe. She began to sing for the second time that day. No sooner had she started than the same yellow bird appeared again and perched on a rock beside her. He had a beautiful golden ring in his beak. He placed the ring on the rock and then sang:

> "Tra-la-la, tra-la-tring
> A song I shall sing
> And for you fair maid
> A gift I shall bring."

66

He once again flew back to the wood, but left the ring. Bawang tried the ring on her finger. It fitted perfectly. As dusk was fast approaching, she returned to the house where she ate her dinner and went to bed.

The next day was as bright as the day before. Bawang once again felt the desire to sing. And, yet again, the yellow bird appeared, this time carrying in its beak a gold bracelet set with diamonds and rubies. Before flying away, he sang:
> "Tra-la-la, tra-la-tring
> A song I shall sing
> And for you fair maid
> A gift I shall bring."

By nightfall he had brought her another gift, this time a necklace studded with sapphires and pearls. And so it went on for seven days until Bawang was covered from head to toe in gold and gems.

By the end of the seventh day, Bawang had become so worried about the old woman that she decided to return to the temple to pray for her safety. No sooner had she knelt to pray than she felt a light touch on her shoulder and knew her guardian had reappeared.

Bawang took her wrinkled hand in hers and cried with joy. And then an amazing thing happened. There was a loud snort and whinny, and Bawang looked up to see a beautiful white stallion.

The young girl knew that this horse would carry her away. Hugging the old woman, Bawang thanked her for her kindness. She began to tell her about the golden-yellow bird and tried to give her some of the jewels, but the woman hushed her and would have nothing. She simply told Bawang that what she wore was rightly hers.

Finally, the old woman told Bawang she had nothing to fear and that the horse would carry her safely to the edge of the forest. They held each other for one last brief moment, then Bawang mounted the stallion and set off on her journey.

But where was she to go? She couldn't return home as they would not welcome her back. And how would she tell them of her adventures? Would they believe her? She decided that she would go and stay with her grandmother who lived in a small house on the outskirts of the village.

Her mind made up, she rested more easily in the saddle. On they swept through glades and thickets, over hills and streams, until her trusty steed came to a stop and waited for her to dismount. No sooner had her feet touched the ground than he reared his head and galloped off into the distance.

Bawang looked around her and saw a familiar landmark. She was back near her village. She struck out across the fields and just before midnight she came to her grandmother's house. She banged on the door and it was several minutes before she heard a stirring inside.

Her grandmother asked in a worried voice: "Who's there? Who's waking me at this time of night?"

"It is me, Bawang!" replied the girl.

"That cannot be," answered her grandmother, "Bawang is dead. She's been eaten by the wild beasts of the forest."

Bawang persisted and soon the old woman opened her door. She gasped with delight when she saw her beautiful granddaughter standing there, and fell back a step when she saw the sparkling jewels.

"Come in, child," she said softly. "Tell me all that has happened to you over these past weeks."

Bawang's grandmother had always believed her to be the better of the two sisters and as her granddaughter told her amazing tale, she now knew for sure that it was true. She understood that the spirit had helped her and given her the jewels because she was a good and truthful girl.

So she invited her to stay for as long as she liked.

Her grandmother then told Bawang that, since she had left, her mother had found it difficult to manage without her. And she had also become angry with Suna, whom she found incapable of completing her duties.

Bawang realized the truth of all that had occurred and how her elder sister had deceived everyone. But being a kind soul, she felt only compassion and a great need to set matters right within her family.

At last the pair went to bed. Bawang slept well but was awoken by a screeching sound at the door. Her grandmother opened up and there stood Suna. She had been sent to fetch some coffee which the old woman roasted and ground herself.

When Bawang also got up to greet her sister, Suna stared at her in surprise.

"Why, I can hardly believe my eyes!" she exclaimed. "Surely it cannot be! It is my own dear sister. You have no idea how upset and worried we have been since you disappeared. Wherever did you go?"

Before Bawang had the chance to reply, Suna continued: "How beautiful you are. Wherever did you come by such lovely jewels?"

Bawang once again recounted her adventures. But Suna kept interrupting her, wanting to know only about the jewelry. In fact she barely heard a word until Bawang spoke about the golden-yellow bird.

"What a wonderful story," she said. "But I really must be going. Mother will be waiting for me." She flounced out of the house, breaking into a run the moment she got past the gate. In her haste, she forgot all about the coffee.

But Suna didn't return home. She wasted no time in retracing Bawang's steps. Before long she was at the river and by nightfall she came to the cave. She walked through it impatiently until she reached the temple that Bawang had described. She sat there waiting expectantly but nothing happened. Unlike her sister, she did not pray in the temple. Exhausted by the long hike, she soon fell into a deep sleep.

When she awoke, she found herself in a small house. Finding fresh clothes at the bottom of her bed, she put them on and then helped herself to some porridge from a simmering pot. Her thoughts turned quickly to the golden-yellow bird. She was about to go out to try to find it when the door opened and the old woman entered.

"And who may you be, you old crow!" she barked.

The good lady softly explained that this was her house and that she had found Suna at the temple and brought her home to protect her from the animals of the forest.

"Well, you cared for my sister, so you can do the same for me!" she demanded loudly and ungraciously and stormed out of the room, her only thought being to find the golden-yellow bird.

The old woman looked sad, but then she knew everything. And so did the bird.

Suna never saw the woman again. Nor did she ever set eyes on the magical bird. Having spent the day looking for it, she returned to the hut shortly before dusk. She finished off the food in the house and sat with her arms folded wondering what to do next. All of a sudden, she heard a beating of wings. Looking up, she saw not a golden-yellow bird, but a huge coal-black crow.

Thinking that, as this was a bigger bird than the one Bawang described, it would be sure to fetch bigger jewels, Suna said: "Off you go, you ugly bird. Go and fetch me some beautiful jewelry. And make sure you get me more than my sister."

The crow looked down at Suna and, in a flurry of wings, flew towards her, ready to attack with his sharp beak. He let out a loud caw and was joined by five more of the biggest crows you can imagine. Before long they were all chasing Suna around the small hut as she screamed and tried to beat them away with her arms. This terrible scene went on for a very long time. Until, that is, the large birds had pecked out Suna's eyes.

Meanwhile, Bawang had gone home and made peace with her mother. But days passed with no sign of Suna. Bawang became anxious for her safety, and set out in search of her. After all, she had been gone ten days now.

Bawang realized where her sister had gone. So once again, she made the trip down the river, along the path, down the steps and through the cave. As she entered, she heard a distant, high-pitched wail that chilled her to her very bones. She was very afraid.

The further into the cave she went, the louder the din became. At last the circle of light appeared; Bawang found herself at the foot of the steps leading towards the glade.

The terrible sounds grew louder as she climbed. What kind of monster was this? As she reached the top of the steps, Bawang froze. Crawling on the floor was Suna. She was blind and in a terrible state. It was she who had been making the wailing noises.

Bawang went to her. As she placed her arms around her sister, Suna recoiled in horror. It was all Bawang could do to convince her she had not come to harm her.

As Bawang gazed at the poor creature, she felt the spirit of the old woman come to her and she was full of divine power. She spoke to her sister in an unearthly voice. And suddenly her sister opened her eyes and could see again.

"Oh Bawang," she cried. "It is you. How stupid and cruel I have been. I cannot tell you the horrors that have befallen me. Please take me away from here."

Taking the frail figure gently in her arms, Bawang led her down the steps through the cave and back to the river's edge. Slowly they made their way home.

Suna never spoke of what happened to her during the time she was away. But the two sisters were reunited in happiness within the family. At night, Suna would sometimes have nightmares where she would toss and turn, as if trying to protect herself from attack. Yet she was a changed person—for the better. She bustled about the yard, always willing to help with the daily chores.

But she never forgot the crow. And Bawang never forgot the golden-yellow bird.

The Four Naughty Boys

Old father Seliweg had four sons with names that sounded nearly the same: Gopling, Goplang, Goplung and Gopleng. He also had a problem—four problems, in fact. His boys were all very naughty.

Seliweg was a carpenter, a master of his craft. His day was spent carving temple doors, making planks for wooden houses and cutting coconut trunks into poles. When his work was finished for the day, he would sit quietly in his back yard and carve blocks of ebony or tangled tree roots into frogs, crickets and all manner of creatures.

Lovingly and proudly, he watched his sons grow up—from the day they were born, through their first playful years to their present youth.

But something had gone wrong. His sons had become rude and unruly. They didn't respect their elders and they were always fighting with each other. Not a day passed without some huge argument. Gopling would hit Goplang, Goplang would attack Goplung, Goplung would punch Gopleng, and Gopleng would biff Gopling. And sometimes all four of them would get into such a terrible fight that the peace of the family home would be shattered.

"Why have they become so unmanageable?" Seliweg wondered sadly.

They had never wanted for love or care or any of life's necessities. Perhaps a sister might have made them more caring towards each other, he thought. Or maybe they had been influenced by the village bully, Semug Bangsel, who lived just down the road. Seliweg racked his brains for a plausible reason.

Seliweg concluded that it was his own fault. Over the years he had spent too much time making animals out of bits of wood rather than spending time caring for his own children.

He sighed, his chin resting in his palm as he looked up at the stars in the calm stillness of the night.

All of a sudden he heard a racket coming from the kitchen. Such shouting and screaming led him to think there was a riot going on in the house.

As he got to his feet he thought it possible that some children were naughtier than others. But then his were far too naughty and had to be taught a lesson.

When he reached the kitchen door, he grabbed a broom made out of stiff twigs and stood in the doorway for a moment. Inside, a battle was raging. Pots and pans clattered onto the floor and dishes flew across the room, as the four boys grabbed anything they could find for missiles in the great battle.

"Silence!" Seliweg shouted in a loud voice he hardly knew he possessed, the broom raised above his head.

The din stopped immediately as the boys pressed back against the wall. They had never heard their father yell like this before. He had never raised so much as a finger against them, and now he held a broom in his hand. They all felt very nervous.

Seliweg stood there glowering at them for a long while.

"Line up, you young troublemakers," he said gruffly, "and, one by one, go outside and stand in the yard. I have something to show you."

The boys did as they were told and waited in anticipation of some awful punishment. Seliweg followed bcind with thc broom, and then spoke to them.

"Gopling, Goplang, Goplung, Gopleng. It seems to me that you are each trying to prove that you are stronger than your brother. Well, if it is a test of strength you want, then a test of strength you shall have."

The boys nodded tentatively, still unsure of their father's intentions.

Seliweg said: "See this broom I have here in my hand?"

He lifted the big bundle of twigs that was bound tightly with bamboo at one end.

"I want each of you to take this broom and try to break it—beginning with you, Gopling," he said as he passed it to his eldest son.

Gopling looked puzzled, but he took the broom and tried to break it across his knee. The bundle would not even bend. After wrestling with it for several minutes, Gopling became so exhausted that he gave up.

Goplang was next, but he, too, admitted defeat after a long struggle. Goplung was next, but he fared no better. Finally, Gopleng, having watched his elder brothers fail, saw no point in even attempting the task.

"Tell us, Father," he said. "Is it possible at all to break the broom without the use of a saw?'

"Of course it is possible!" Seliweg replied. "Watch closely and I will show you how." Carefully he untied the bamboo binding, and very slowly separated the twigs and started snapping them one by one. The boys watched their father wide-eyed, with open-mouthed wonder.

When Seliweg had finished and all the twigs lay broken at his feet, he said: "Let this be a lesson to you all. If you all stand together, like the switches in a broom, you will be strong together. If you are divided and work against each other, then you will be weak and sure to fail in life."

Luckily the boys heeded their father's advice. They worked in harmony from then on, and all eventually became master carpenters themselves.

The Missing Pig

A poor family with five sons lived in a small mountain village in Bali. The boys were all strong and healthy, but the oldest was a little simple in the mind. He had a good heart, but was always getting in a muddle. His name was Wayan.

In Bali, all children are named in the order of their birth. The first born is Wayan, the second child is Madé, the third is Nyoman and the fourth is Ketut. The order is repeated when there are more children.

Now, as you can imagine, in a compound where aunts, uncles, grannies, granddads, mothers, fathers and all their children live, this naming system can get very confusing. Call out "Wayan", and more than one person is sure to answer.

This particular slow-witted Wayan was known as Wayan Dokok, which was often shortened to Dokok.

Although Dokok was a simple child, his mother and father lavished love, time and care on him—even more than they did their other four sons. But there were times when Dokok's behaviour severely tested their patience. The other siblings, sometimes jealous of Dokok's special treatment, would encourage him in his misadventures, egging him on so that he would often get a telling-off from his parents later.

Once the family had a ceremonial feast and Dokok tried dried eel for the first time—a special treat. He had never tasted anything so delicious. When he had eaten his serving, he wanted some more. But, sadly, the eels were all finished.

One of his younger brothers leaned over and said slyly: "I know where there are more of these delicious things."

Dokok's eyes lit up. He was still hungry—in fact, he was always hungry.

Madé led him into the kitchen and pointed to the rafters, which were tied with lengths of black string, the curly loose ends dangling. To Dokok they looked like the twisty black eels he had earlier enjoyed so much. He needed no further encouragement.

Climbing up to the roof on a ladder, he tugged out and tore down every little strand of string he could lay his hands on. Soon he had amassed a whole pile of straggly bits of string. Impatient to tuck into his feast, he leapt heavily from the roof. As he did so, he heard a loud splintering crack and the roof fell onto his head.

Everyone rushed into the kitchen to see Dokok emerging from the rubble with a silly grin on his face and black string between his teeth. His parents were furious and sent Dokok straight to bed.

At another time, while the rice was being harvested, Dokok's mother asked her son to take the flock of family ducks to the rice fields to feed on the small water animals that lived there. All he had to do was keep an eye on them while they foraged, then bring them safely home. Nothing could be simpler—or so she thought.

The boy led the way using a little banner of white cloth tied to the end of a bamboo pole. The ducks followed in a straight line until they arrived at the banks of the flooded field. Dokok planted the pole in the ground, certain that the ducks would not wander away.

He sat down as the ducks swam and splashed about. But as Dokok watched, he thought that they looked thin.

"How could they possibly get enough to eat?" Dokok wondered. After all, only small fishes, tadpoles and worms lived in the cloudy water.

Dokok had an idea (which was always dangerous). He would take the ducks to the river instead. He knew that river was deep and wide and was full of fat fish. His ducks would have a feast there.

He jumped to his feet and grabbed the pole. The ducks quickly assembled again and, in single file, followed him to the river. There, they seemed to enjoy themselves better. Dokok laughed as he watched them going "*Quack! Quack! Quack!*"

Then Dokok noticed that none of the ducks were catching any fish. Perhaps the fish were resting on the bottom, he thought. He had another idea: he would help the ducks get their dinner.

So he grabbed each of the birds and attached rocks to their feet using thin slivers of bamboo. He then threw them back in the river, and happily watched them vanish beneath the surface of the water.

Time drifted by, and Dokok lazed on the sunlit bank imagining the chase going on in the water below.

"Those ducks must be having a fine old time," he thought to himself. "Why, they would soon have finished off every fish in the river!"

He laughed and laughed, rolling about on the bank, slapping his sides until he accidentally tumbled into the water. He stood up in the water and felt something soft and squishy beneath his fee   He bent down to see what it was and pulled up a drowned duck. Soon he had found a whole pyramid of the poor birds, all dead.

But Dokok was not worried at all. Quite the opposite, in fact, as there would be roast duck for everyone for days on end. Just the thought of it made him hungry.

He arrived home, whistling, dead ducks hanging from both ends of his herdsmen's pole slung across his shoulders. But he didn't get the warm welcome he was expecting. His mother was furious. So was his father. The other boys laughed their heads off, and this tale kept them amused for weeks.

Quite a long time passed before Wayan Dokok was given any more jobs either indoors or out. But the day came when his mother needed to go out to do some shopping. All the other senior members of the family were also out, so she had no choice but to leave the boys on their own.

She felt rather sorry for her eldest son who had sensed that he was good for nothing. In fact, he had become very quiet of late and wasn't eating as much as he usually did. So, before leaving, she took Dokok by the hand and led him out to the backyard.

There she pointed to the pigs—a fat sow and her litter of ten piglets—and asked him to watch over them while she was away.

"There are ten piglets here, Dokok," she said. "I expect there to be ten when I come back."

Dokok immediately felt much better. He grinned from ear to ear. His mother was relieved to see her son cheerful once more and left happily, sure that nothing could go wrong.

"Funny things, pigs," thought Dokok, as he watched them scamper here and there, snuffling, snorting and squealing, their curly tails wiggling all the while. "And so good to eat!"

His appetite had returned. For a few moments, he pretended to be a pig himself. He crawled around on all fours, imitating the animals' grunting noises. But the pigs were afraid of him. And he was soon covered from head-to-toe in mud.

When his brothers started laughing, he stopped.

"Why do you always make fun of me?" he asked them.

He once again sat watching the pigs. He twiddled his thumbs, he whistled to himself, he swatted the odd fly. But soon he was bored again.

"I know," he thought to himself, "I will count the pigs."

Eyes crinkled, and using his fingers and thumbs, he slowly began to count. "One pig. Two pigs. Three pigs. Four pigs . . . " One of the piglets ran behind a bush. So he started again.

"One. Two. Three. Four. Five . . . " Then several of the little pigs huddled together and he lost count. He started over once again.

"One pig. Two pigs. Three pigs . . . " This counting went on for a long time because it was hard to count pigs running around in the yard.

At last Dokok counted to ten. "Hang on a minute," he hesitated. "There's one extra pig. But that cannot be."

He started again and reached the same answer. There weren't just ten pigs—there was another one. But what came after ten? Dokok looked down at his fingers and thumbs and racked his brain.

"Why, nothing comes after ten," he said to himself. Ten was the biggest number, he was certain of that.

And so he thought, in his simple way, if there was nothing after ten, then that additional pig had no right to be there at all.

There was only one solution. As his tummy rumbled, Dokok decided that the extra pig that shouldn't be there should be roasted.

If there was one thing Wayan Dokok knew how to do properly, it was roasting a pig. All his brothers knew this. And although they offered no help in capturing the pig, lighting the fire, or turning the spit, they certainly encouraged him in his work.

And when the air was heavy with the smell of roast pork, they were there to help him eat it. In fact, soon enough there was nothing left but a curly little pig's tail. Dokok realized that the smart thing to do would be to hide the remains of their feast from their mother.

But what would he do with the tail?

He asked his brothers for advice and they soon came up with the idea that Dokok should hide it down his trousers. So the brothers got together, turned Dokok around and stuffed it down the back of his pants.

They suppressed their giggles when they noticed a small hole in seat of the threadbare garment, through which the end of the tail popped out. Poor Dokok; he had no idea what was going on.

As far as he was concerned, he couldn't see the tail so it no longer existed: out of sight, out of mind.

Not long afterwards, the boys' mother returned from her shopping trip. She saw Dokok in the yard, and smiled at him and asked if he had been a good boy. He nodded and grinned back. His mother did not notice anything amiss then, because Dokok stood facing her all the while.

It was the pigs' feeding time and Dokok's mother fetched a bucket of swill. As she came towards them, the pigs raced over to the trough. As they crowded around and began to eat, Dokok's mother thought she would check that the pigs were all there. She counted them once; she counted them twice; she counted them three times.

"WAYAN DOKOK!" she shouted at the top of her voice. Dokok heard his name being called and knew he was in trouble again.

"There were eleven pigs when I left. But there are not eleven now," she raved.

"What is eleven?" he asked. "There are ten pigs," he said as he counted one to ten on his fingers.

"Dokok, there were ten piglets and one sow which makes eleven," said his mother. "Ten plus one is eleven."

He nodded his head, but he didn't understand what his mother meant.

"Where is the missing piglet?" his mother asked.

Dokok was too afraid to answer and turned around to run inside the house. As he did, his mother spied the pig's tail sticking out of his trousers. Despite her anger, she couldn't help but laugh.

Dokok looked at her, glad to see her mood change, and laughed as well—although he had no idea what was so funny.

His mother then called his brothers Madé, Ketut, Nyoman and Wayan the younger. She gave them such a telling off, not only for eating the roast pig but also for making fun of their brother.

After that, Wayan Dokok was taught to count from one to twenty.

The Three Fishes

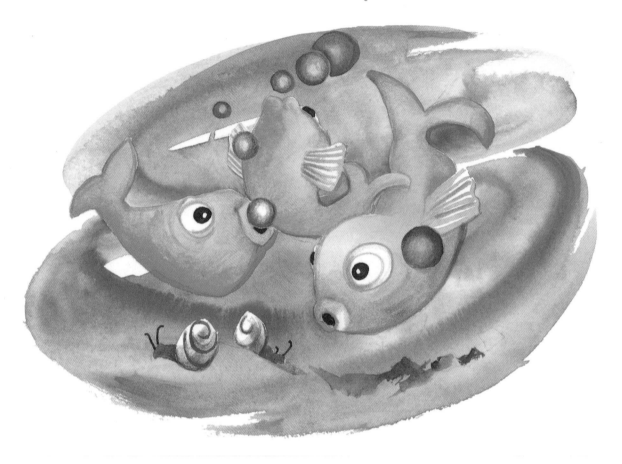

Once upon a time, there were three fishes who lived happily in a lily pond next to a rice field. The pond was in the garden of a small bamboo house that was rented out to tourists who came to stay in Bali. The local people wouldn't dream of living next to the rice paddies, but the foreigners seemed to like it.

In the pond grew some beautiful pink and white lilies that bloomed at night. And the fish had plenty to eat, what with the slugs and snails and small water creatures that lived there. Sometimes, the guests in the house would even feed them breadcrumbs.

But one day the most terrible thing happened. It had been very hot and there hadn't been any rain for months. The water in the pond had got very low indeed. In fact, all that remained was just a few inches of warm, brown muddy water, barely enough to keep the fishes alive.

The fish got together and talked about what they could do. The first fish, who was the oldest, said that he wanted to stay put. He was sure that there would be rain soon. And if not, he believed that the owner of the house would see the terrible state of the pond and fill it up with fresh water.

The second fish agreed, but wasn't quite as sure as the first. The third fish who was the youngest had an altogether different plan. He had noticed the channel of water running down the side of the rice field. There was always water there, he reasoned, as it was needed for the rice crop. And, who knows, it might even lead to the stream in the gully below. All he would have to do was make one great giant leap, and he would be there, soon to swim to freedom.

The first fish thought the plan far too dangerous. What if he didn't jump far enough? He would be stranded on the ground where he would quickly die. And what if the channel wasn't connected to the stream. The channel was very shallow and muddy. It would be very easy for a bird to spy him there and gobble him up.

No, it was a very bad plan indeed. His advice to the younger fish was to be patient and stay put.

But the second fish didn't agree at all. And before you could say jumping jack flash he took one giant leap out of the muddy brown pond. The other two fish looked on as he flew up into the air, winging his way towards the rice field on the other side of the garden path.

Then splat! The poor little fish didn't have enough power in his little fins to take him all the way to the channel. And there he lay slap bang in the middle of the path. The other two fishes could hear him flapping about.

Then they heard him cry: "Help! Help! Somebody please help me!"

The other two fishes could do nothing to help their friend. And besides, they had enough problems of their own. As they swam in the tiny pool of water left in the pond they were very sad indeed.

Then suddenly they heard voices. It was the tourists who were staying in the house. As they walked along the path, the girl said: "Oh look. There's a fish out of water. Let's help it."

"He must have come from our pond," said the boy, as he picked up the fish in his hand. Gently he placed the stranded fish back into the muddy brown water. "This pond looks pretty dry to me," he said, "looks like it could do with a refill. Let's get some buckets of water from the kitchen."

Much to the relief of the three fishes the pond was soon full of water, and life returned to normal. Of course the older fish couldn't resist giving the younger fish a bit of a telling off. "You really must look before you leap," he told his young friend. "You had a very narrow escape. If the tourists hadn't found you when they did, you would surely have perished."

The young fish blew some bubbles out of his mouth and agreed. Secretly though he thought he had saved the day with his reckless jump. If the tourists hadn't found him they would never have noticed that the pool needed filling up.

Or would they?

Other children's titles from Tuttle Publishing and Periplus Editions:

Filipino Children's Favorite Stories
Retold by Liana Romulo
Illustrated by Joanne de Leon

These popular myths and tales from the Philippines, together with the beautiful watercolor illustrations by award-winning Joanne de Leon, will enchant six- to ten-year-old readers from all over the world. This is a must-have book for all children.

Periplus Editions
ISBN 962-593-765-X
120 pages, US$16.95, hardcover

Japanese Children's Favorite Stories
Edited by Florence Sakade
Illustrated by Yoshisuke Kurosaki

"Truly a gem for any library. Destined to give joy to children in every land; sure to create sympathetic understanding."
—Roanoke Times

Tuttle Publishing
ISBN 0-8048-0284-X
120 pages, US$16.95, hardcover

Tales of a Chinese Grandmother
By Francis Carpenter
Illustrated by Malthe Hasselriis

A rich collection of Chinese folklore stories told by grand-mother Lao Lao to Yu Lang and Ah Shung, whose curiosity and love for stories mark their kinship with children the world over.

Tuttle Publishing
ISBN 0-8048-1042-7
302 pages, US$11.95, paperback

Favorite Children's Stories from China and Tibet
By Lotta Carswell Hume
Illustrated by Lo Koonchiu

"These are excellent stories and should hold the attention of the younger set for hours if your voice holds out."
—Sacramento Bee

Tuttle Publishing
ISBN 0-8048-3303-6
120 pages, US$16.95, hardcover

Little One Inch
Edited by Florence Sakade
Illustrated by Yoshisuke Kurosaki

This volume brings together many of Japan's best loved children's stories that have been enjoyed by generations of children.

Tuttle Publishing
ISBN 0-8048-0384-6
60 pages, US$9.95, paperback

Tokyo Friends
Edited and illustrated by
Betty Reynolds

This magical book introduces the young reader to Japanese traditions, customs, and language by means of helpful English-Japanese glosses, which augment the delightful, lively narrative.

Tuttle Publishing
ISBN 0-8048-2123-2
64 pages, US$12.95, hardcover